D0475518

You Look Yummy!

TATSUYA MIYANISHI

MUSEYON, New York

a baby Ankylosaurus hatched.
But…

pop!

in the big, big world
he was all alone....
The baby cried,
because he felt lonely.
And as he cried he trudged along,

"Heh heh heh…you look yummy!" a Tyrannosaurus said. He drooled hungrily as he got ready to pounce on the baby Ankylosaurus.

"Daddy!"
The Ankylosaurus grabbed onto
the leg of the Tyrannosaurus.
"I was really lonely. I was scared."

The Tyrannosaurus was stunned!
He blurted out,
"Why do you think I'm your da-da-daddy?"

"You just called my name, didn't you?
You know my name
'cause you're my daddy, right?"

"Your name?"

"Yes. You said,
'You look YUMMY!'
My name is Yummy, isn't it?"

As the Tyrannosaurus gave
him a blank look…

"Ah, I'm so hungry," said Yummy,
and he started munching on grass.
"It's good! Why don't you eat too, Daddy?"

"Umm…I like meat better than grass…"
the Tyrannosaurus said.
"No, Daddy isn't really hungry. You eat it all."

"Thank you. I'm gonna eat a lot because
I wanna be big JUST LIKE YOU, Daddy."

"Uh…you want to be like me?"
the Tyrannosaurus mumbled to himself quietly.
Just then…

a Chilantaisaurus approached
with hungry, greedy eyes.
"Hee, hee, hee…he looks yummy."

"You know me too, mister?"

"Sure, I do. I know you very well.
Because you look YUMMY!"
As soon as he finished talking,
the Chilantaisaurus popped open
his big mouth and pounced on Yummy.

Gulp!

"Mmmph...."
The Tyrannosaurus protected Yummy.
He swung his tail, even though he felt
the pain of the Chilantaisaurus's attack.

THWACK!

Thwack!
Yummy was so busy munching on the grass, he didn't even see what happened.

Once he finished eating the grass,
Yummy fell asleep peacefully.

Looking at Yummy,
the Tyrannosaurus mumbled,
"He wants to be just like me...."
Even more than the wound in his back,
his heart ached throughout the night.

The next morning, a volcano erupted.

Boom!

The noise woke the Tyrannosaurus.
Yummy wasn't there with him.
"Where did that little thing go?"
The Tyrannosaurus wandered around,
looking for Yummy.
He looked behind a rock,
in the pond, in the woods,
and in the grass....
"What if that Chilantaisaurus
from yesterday..." he thought.

Just then he heard,
"Daddy!"

When he turned around,
he found Yummy walking toward him,
carrying red berries on his back.

"Eat these, Daddy.
You don't like grass, do you?
So I went to the mountain over there
and picked these berries for you.
I did a good job, didn't I?"

"Wh-why did you go that far?
It's dangerous, you know!"
the Tyrannosaurus scolded Yummy.

"I'm…I'm sorry, Daddy.
I thought you would be happy…
I'm so sorry," Yummy cried.

"I...I understand now.
It's okay. Please don't cry...."
Saying that, the Tyrannosaurus
tossed a red berry into his mouth.
"Um...yum. Thank you,
Yummy. It's delicious."

From then on, Yummy went to get red berries for the Tyrannosaurus every morning.

Soon, the Tyrannosaurus
started teaching
Yummy many things.

"Look, Yummy.
This is ramming."

They spent day after day
together this way.

Then, one evening,
the Tyrannosaurus said to Yummy,
"I taught you everything I could,
Yummy. So, it's time to say
goodbye now."

"Okay! I won't lose."
Wiping away his tears,
Yummy started running.
He ran as fast as he could.
He ran straight to the mountain.
"I'm gonna be with my daddy
forever and ever!"
Yummy never looked back and
kept running, running, running....

"Goodbye, Yummy…"
the Tyrannosaurus whispered.
And he popped a red berry
into his mouth.

YOU LOOK YUMMY!

Omae Umasou dana © 2003 Tatsuya Miyanishi
All rights reserved.

Translation by Mariko Shii Gharbi
English editing by Heather Corcoran and Janice Battiste

Published in the United States and Canada by:
Museyon Inc.
1177 Avenue of the Americas, 5th Floor
New York, NY 10036

Museyon is a registered trademark.
Visit us online at www.museyon.com

Originally published in Japan in 2003 by POPLAR Publishing Co., Ltd.
English translation rights arranged with POPLAR Publishing Co., Ltd.

Printed in Shenzhen, China

ISBN 978-1-940842-06-6